Sage

God Will Provide

Sage Series Book 2

Written by

Belinda K Owens

Copyright © 2019 Belinda Owens
All rights reserved.

DEDICATION

The dedication of this book is to my husband who has supported me on the journey to find my heritage. He has always believed in me and encouraged me in all my endeavors.

It had been a cold winter. It seemed as though the snow had come quickly. After a summer full of playing in this Ozark valley, and helping grandma with the garden, Sage was ready for some slowing down. She loved setting in the window of the log cabin watching the snow fall against the moonlight. Winter had arrived in the Ozark Mountains.

Grandpa had given Sage a new pony for her birthday back in the fall. He was a brown color just like the color of the oak leaves as they change color and then fall to the ground. Bullet was brown with a blonde mane and tail. Sage thought he was the prettiest pony in the whole world.

Sage named her pony Bullet. She would set high on his back as she rode him out of the corral gate. Oh my, how she loved riding Bullet and he loved the adventure of running over the Ozark hills! Bullet seemed to fit for his name as Sage thought he was the fastest horse around! She would pass thru the gate and off they would go over the hills and down in the valley! Now that winter had arrived Sage and Bullet were both missing those long adventures.

As the snow fell Sage was all curled up in the window watching Bullet as he stood in the barn. The snow fell as big white flakes covering the ground. Sage was all warm curled up by the crackling fireplace. Even though winter was a time for staying indoors Sage still dreamed of heading out of the barn on Bullet's back.

Winter meant evenings spent listening to Grandpa talk about the crops he would plant as soon as spring came. In the spring and summer, Grandpa is always so busy that Sage doesn't get that special time with him. He has a lot to get done planting seeds then tending the crops all the way up to harvest time.

"I think we need to plant more corn this spring," Grandpa said to Grandma. "These winters just keep getting colder and longer, seems like we run real close on having enough food for all the animals." Grandma was setting in her rocker knitting Sage a new sweater. "Yeah that would probably be a wise thing to do," Grandma said. "It's better to have a little extra than to run out."

About that time Sage turned from looking out the window. She said, "Grandpa, tell me what it was like when you were a boy." Grandpa leaned back in his chair and thought, "well Sage, when I was a boy it was different. I always helped my grandpa every year. We lived in a different kind of house back then. I even helped to build ours. They were kind of round on top, built with straw and sticks. They were called wigwams."

"We would gather straw and when we had enough we would make our wigwam. It made a good strong house. It was a little bit different than this log cabin you live in," Grandpa said. "Our floors were dirt and here in this cabin you have wood to stand on." Sage was picturing what the house must have been like.

Powhatan House also known as a wigwam

Grandpa continued talking to Sage, "we would go out and hunt a lot as I do now except back then there were many of us and we would go together in a hunting party," Grandpa said.

"I remember one time it seemed like we were going to run out of food. The winter had been very cold. I think the animals eat more when it is colder. I guess they have to eat to make their body warm. Food was running out and the winter was a very hard one. We had lots of snow. I don't think I had ever seen so much snow."

"One winter my father was so concerned because the snow and cold had just stayed longer than usual. I remember he gathered us all together, everyone in our tribe. You do know my father, your great grandfather, was a Chief right? Well, he called us all together and then he said "We are running out of food. The snow has stayed way longer than it should have. We have nowhere to turn but I want to try something," Great Grandpa the Chief said.

"I heard a story about a man who lived long ago," Great Grandpa said. "He needed to feed his people. This man I heard of they called him Jesus. He was the leader of his tribe. They say he had just five loaves of bread and only two fish so he prayed and he had his men pass it out to his people."

"They say he was the Son of God, the Son of our Creator. I was told that he fed his people all they wanted with just the fish and bread. I as your Chief want to try this." As my father stood tall before his people he said "this Jesus we have heard of multiplied two fish and five loaves, if you Jesus can hear me please multiply our food, our meat, and our corn. Help my people to not starve". "That winter our food never ran out. Every time we went into the storehouse there was more. We ate well all the rest of the winter. This Jesus had helped our people," Grandpa said.

Powhatan storehouse

"So I truly believe the story in that bible where it says he fed the people with two fish and five loaves of bread. From that time on I have always thanked God or Creator for all that he has given to us. Why I even thanked him for old Bullet out there!" Sage glanced out the window at Bullet then she turned toward Grandma and said, "I thank him for Bullet, and I thank him for Grandma and you Grandpa! I am even thankful for my beautiful sweater Grandma is making just for me!"

"You know God our Creator loves it when we are thankful. I thank him for all we have right here in this valley. From this log cabin to every corn and pea we raise. God, you are good to me," Grandma said. "I could never thank him enough for giving me you, Sage. I believe God made you just for me & Grandpa."

The End

Made in the USA
Columbia, SC
11 August 2020